a greene family christmas

piper rayne

about a greene family christmas

Preparing a Christmas to remember is no small feat with a family the size of the Greenes.

Especially when the woman who has always been the planner down to every minute detail, falls ill only five days before the holiday. The family has no choice but to scramble to ensure that nothing is amiss. Cookies need to be decorated, gingerbread houses assembled and decorations to be hung. They'll need all hands on deck, both young and old, to make this holiday happen. But of course, what would a Greene Christmas be if not chaotic with a dash of drama?

a greene family CHRISTMAS

<u>**The Greenes**</u>

<u>**Hank's Kids**</u>
Cade Greene (49)
Co-owner Truth or Dare Brewery
Fisher Greene (47)
Sheriff
Xavier Greene (45)
Pro Football Player
Adam Greene (43)
Forest Ranger
Chevelle Greene (42)
Water Boat Tourist

<u>**Marla's Kids**</u>
Jed Greene (49)
Co-owner of Truth or Dare Brewery
Nikki Greene (46)
Radio Host
Mandi Greene (44)
Owner of SunBay Inn
Posey Greene (40)
Owner of Fringe

<u>**Hank and Marla's Kid**</u>
Rylan Greene (29)

HANK

After elbowing my way through the grocery store for the past hour, I return home, anxious to sit on the couch and watch the Monday night football game.

"Okay, I think I got everything you need," I holler to Marla when I get inside the house. The holiday music is playing, so I have no idea if she heard me or not.

Christmas is her favorite holiday, and she goes all out on every inch of our house. Now that we're grandparents to twenty-two grandchildren, every year she's adding more and more to the to-do list, trying to top the previous year. Even when I tell her it's not about the presents or the perfectly baked sugar cookies or the structurally sound gingerbread house, it's that we're blessed to be together another year, she insists on making a fuss.

She understands what the holiday is really all about, but my wife loves to see everyone's reactions. She's addicted to their hugs and smiles.

I set the bags on the kitchen table, hoping this will be my last trip to the grocery store until after Christmas. Today was my third trip in two days. Christmas is only five days away, so there's lots of time for her to figure out something else she's missing.

"Marla!" I shout when she doesn't join me in the kitchen.

No answer, so I unload the groceries, putting the cold

items away first. Then I spot her walking down the hallway and leaning against the doorframe as though she ran a marathon and worries her legs might give out. She looks off.

"Honey, what's wrong?" I walk over to her and lead her to a chair.

"Remember how Isaiah and Sam caught that flu going around last week?"

Xavier and Clara's twin boys just entered kindergarten and are going through that horrible phase of catching every germ imaginable. Since Marla pretty much runs the after-school pickup for the Greene family so that all the parents can continue working the rest of the day, her immune system is relearning it all too. She's been sick more this year than any other.

"Please tell me you're not sick again?"

She nods. "I felt off this morning but figured it was that I'm getting older. Too old to be doing all this." She motions toward the bags of groceries I've yet to unpack.

"Exactly my point the other night." When I was giving her a foot massage until she fell asleep at seven o'clock.

She shakes her head. "Christmas is what brings family together. I wouldn't have it any other way. It's part of what's made us one family, not two."

I open my mouth to argue, but I've learned a lot during my married years, and now is not the time. And I can't fault Marla. Her one goal ever since we got married has been to make sure every single person in our blended family feels as though they belong.

"Let's get you to bed."

"No!" She tries to stand but has to grip the table to steady herself. She inhales deeply.

"I'm not taking no for an answer." I sweep my bride up in my arms, and she wraps her arms around my neck, her eyes already slipping shut. She's running herself ragged.

I walk up the stairs, which is admittedly harder to do than

it was a decade ago, bring her to our master bedroom, and lay her down on the bed. First, I remove her socks and her pants, leaving her in her panties and shirt, then slide her under the blankets. I press a kiss to her forehead. "Sleep well, honey. I'll be up to check on you in a little bit."

She murmurs, fighting sleep, but she's out by the time I shut the door.

I'm walking downstairs toward the kitchen when I hear someone come in through the garage door.

"Ry?" I ask.

"Hey, Dad." He drops his bag and looks around. "Where's Mom?"

"Where's Mom?" I ask, opening my arms. "Give your ol' man a hug."

He walks into my arms, and I hold him tightly. I barely see my youngest son anymore now that he's a professional soccer player. And it isn't as if he can't come visit. He has plenty of time in the off-season, but I feel like he doesn't want to come home very often. I have my suspicions as to why, but I keep those to myself. He'll open up to me eventually.

"It's good to have you home."

We step out of the embrace, and I take him in. Rylan's more muscular than ever, conditioned and toned to play the sport he loves. It's his face that strikes me the most, show-casing the passage of time with how grown up he looks with a five-o'clock shadow and strong jaw.

"So, where's Mom?"

I sigh. "She's sick."

"Sick?" His eyes widen, and he looks toward the stairs.

When I got diagnosed with cancer many years ago, Rylan was still living at home. He saw me day in and day out, and I think it scared him more than he ever let on.

"No." I shake my head before he thinks the worst. "Xavier's twins brought something home from school. She's sleeping." I walk into the kitchen to continue unloading the groceries. "If she doesn't beat it fast, I'll need your help."

"You got it," he says, then takes a container of leftovers out of the fridge and fixes himself a plate. He waits by the microwave as I put the groceries away.

"I thought you weren't coming home for a few more days?" I ask, not wanting to pry. It's taken me a lot of kids to realize the more they think you're prying, the more they hide. Best to act like you don't give a shit either way.

"A friend of mine is having a party later this week, but I canceled at the last minute. Just needed to be home."

"Well, I couldn't be happier to see you."

The microwave dings and he sits down at the table with his fork in hand. Then he stands and goes into our laundry room, where our spare fridge is, returning with a water. He's antsy.

I get some of the things organized that I know for sure Marla would want done, trying not to analyze his every move.

"Hey, Dad?"

"Yeah?"

"How come you never left Sunrise Bay?"

Ah, there it is. I think each of my kids has asked me that question at some point in their life. I have to be careful how I respond because first, I need to taper down my own excitement. I'm guessing that if he's asking that question, it means he's contemplating moving back. I've always pushed my kids to try to achieve their dreams, and sometimes those dreams take them far away. But a small piece of me always wishes they'll want to stick around Sunrise Bay and live near us.

"Well..." I take a break, sitting down across the table from him and being a hundred-percent honest with him, hoping it'll help him do some self-reflection and discovery this week while he's home.

Chapter Two

I sit and watch the table of four guys scarf down every crumb of food I spent the morning preparing. You'd think I'd have grown used to this by now, but it's like Logan and a bunch of mini-mes. You'd be hard pressed to find one feature of mine in our three sons.

"Hey, babe, you okay this morning?" Logan lifts his wrist to my forehead.

"I'm fine. Just tired."

The three boys—Noah, Crew, and Wade—get up at the same time, walking their plates to the sink. The dishes are put in along with the empty smoothie glasses that Logan has them drink every morning.

"It's the first day of Christmas break… we could go ice skating or sledding or maybe even skiing?" I offer up some choices other than what Logan has already planned for them —a day away from me.

Okay, yes, I'm being a tad dramatic, but sometimes I feel as though I don't fit into my own family.

"Training first. We'll be off on Christmas." Logan smiles at me, snagging the last piece of bacon as if it's a prize.

"I'll stay with you, Mom." Wade, our youngest, grabs my hand.

That's a subject I need to broach with Logan—Wade might not be the next MMA fighter my husband wants him to be.

Logan comes home and complains about Wade's focus, and Wade tells me it's boring at the gym. Our oldest, Noah, can't get enough of the fighting, but he's always had a lot of restless energy that Wade doesn't.

I run my hand through Wade's blond hair and ruffle it up a little. "Well since you guys are busy, I guess I'll go over to Grandma's to check up on her. But I'll sneak out a few cookies for you."

He smiles.

Each boy says goodbye, Noah now tall enough to tower over me. They all walk out the front door to their dad's truck, which I'm sure Noah will be driving now that he has his permit.

Logan lingers. "Want help with the dishes before we leave?"

I shake my head.

"Is everything… okay?"

I hear his hesitation, and I'm not sure why he can't see the problem. Actually, it infuriates me that he doesn't.

"I'm fine. I'm just going to check on my mom. Hank told me she went to bed early last night and with Christmas… seems odd. I want to make sure everything is okay."

He kisses my cheek then my temple. "All right then… we'll be back later."

"Logs," I say right before he walks out of the kitchen.

He turns to me and smiles. Oh, I fell hard and fast for that man and that amazingly cocky smile.

I shake my head, not wanting to get into all of this while the boys are waiting outside. "Never mind. See you tonight."

"You sure?"

I nod. "Yes, I'm sure. Go."

"Love you," he calls right before I hear the front door shut.

I watch the truck pull away, sulking for a second, before cleaning up the kitchen.

Chip and I have our Christmas Special on Thursday, but

other than that, I'm free. I wanted time with the kids while they were off from school. I doubled up on my podcast interviews during November and early December so that I'd have more time for the boys over the holidays.

Still feeling a little low, I do the dishes, straighten up the beds upstairs, and grab my purse to head over to my mom's place.

———

"Hello!" I shout when I open the door.

Ever since Mom and Hank became empty nesters eleven years ago when Rylan went to college, you have to be careful. They were like horny teenagers those first few years, and my siblings and I have all walked in on our fair share of naked asses over the years.

"Nikki," Hank whispers and waves me into the kitchen. "She's still asleep."

"Seriously?"

My mom is never sick in bed long. She pushes herself to the limit. It's where I got it from.

"Yeah, she's got a fever, and she threw up a couple times last night." Hank raises the pot of coffee in his hand, but I shake my head.

"No thanks. I saw Rylan post a picture at home last night. He's already here?" I sit at the kitchen table.

"Did he send it to you?" Hank asks.

I laugh because he and Mom are kind of removed from the new apps on the phone. "No, I saw it on this new app."

He nods and sips his coffee, joining me at the table. "I quit trying to keep up with the latest and greatest years ago. He's upstairs getting ready because I need him to pick up Trey and Emelia from Lake Starlight."

"Why?"

"Grandma Ethel picked them up from the airport in the

Northern Lights van, but it won't be coming out here." He shrugs. "It's a closer pickup than the airport."

"And Jed and Adam?" I inquire, wondering why their fathers can't get them.

"Work, and Lucy is having her class holiday pageant tonight. Molly has clients she needs to see before they go away on holiday."

"Maybe I'll go with him," I say, needing something to do.

"Well." Hank looks at the ceiling where Rylan's room is. "He's going in a little early. Said he had to stop and see Declan, but I'm not buying it."

"Me either. Did I tell you I ran into her last month?"

Hank shakes his head.

"She looks good."

"Happy?"

I shrug. "She'd probably fake it for me."

"True." Hank sits in silence for a moment. "Anyway, we have to get things together for Christmas. With your mom sick, we need to divide and conquer." He hands me a list of all the items that need to be done.

"Can you get the family together? We'll figure out who can take what from the list to make sure everything is exactly like Mom would've done," I say.

And here I thought maybe this year would be a relaxing Christmas where I wasn't making gingerbread houses and decorating a bazillion cookies. And maybe just this once, I wouldn't have to be embarrassed on our caroling trip down the streets of Sunrise Bay.

Footsteps sound on the stairs, and I know it has to be Rylan from the way they're taking them two at a time. Sure enough, my soccer star younger brother walks into the kitchen.

"Hey, Nik," he says and heads to the fridge, where he grabs a water and an apple.

"That's it? No hug?" I stand.

He chuckles and sets down his water and apple before enveloping me in a hug that makes me feel tiny. I can't believe this… man is my little Ryguy.

"Sorry," he says before stepping back and grabbing the water and apple again. "I'll take Mom's car."

Hank nods.

I look Rylan up and down one more time before he waves and says goodbye.

Once the garage door is shut, I look at Hank. "Cologne and freshly shaved?"

Hank smiles brightly because we've always loved the girl Rylan likes to hide from us. Maybe he's finally back to doing what he should've a long time ago. "If it wasn't for his faded jeans and sweatshirt, I would've thought maybe…"

"He's still in his twenties, Hank. Jeans and a sweatshirt are practically the standard-issue uniform. The cologne says it all."

"What do you think?"

"Make sure you have another place setting for Christmas dinner, just in case."

And for the next half hour, I do something I haven't in a very long time—I catch up with my stepdad, dividing and conquering to make Christmas the extravagant affair it always is because we both love my mother and don't dare disappoint her.

Chapter Three

Calista

"**R**eady for a break?" My dad peeks his head into the back office of his restaurant where I'm reconciling his month end. Usually I'd work at my place, but of course this week my neighbors above had a flood in their apartment that leaked into mine. Now I'm a twenty-nine-year-old crashing at her little brother's place. Good times.

"For?"

"I'm going to get Rhea and Jason from the bus stop. Remember when you'd come home from college?"

I fiddle with my pencil, hating to think about all those years they'd pick me up when I came home from college because *he* was usually there with me. The way our eyes would catch one last time before we headed in different directions.

"I'll see them tonight."

"Come on. Humor me. I never see you anymore." My dad plasters on a huge smile. "Plus, a few of your aunts and uncles will be there too."

I drop my pencil and slide my chair away from the desk. "First off, I live in Lake Starlight. Second, I see everyone all the time."

I grab my coat off the back door hook and slide my arms through the sleeves before zipping it up. Then I pull my beanie and mitts from the pockets and put them on.

"I know, but it's good to get outside for some fresh air every now and then." My dad smiles widely.

I shake my head. He's worried about me. Everyone in my huge-ass family is worried about me. I'm about to be thirty and none of my life goals have panned out. I'm unmarried, with no kids, and while I do own my own business, I'm the sole employee. And on top of that, I live in a small town where I know practically everyone, so my prospects of finding love are slim to none.

We walk out of my dad's restaurant in downtown Lake Starlight, and we both shove our hands into our jacket pockets.

"You know when you found out about me?"

My dad gives me his sideways glance. The one where it's clear he doesn't like the topic. He and my mom had a one-night stand, and he didn't find out about me until I was almost two years old. If not for my mom having no choice but to find my dad because of a medical issue, they might never have found one another and had five more kids together.

Facing forward, he asks, "Are you pregnant?"

"What?" I laugh. "With whose baby? I know it's close to Christmas, but don't expect an immaculate conception."

He shrugs. "I was young once. You know you were conceived from a one-night stand where we didn't get each other's names. Things happen."

"Unfortunately, yes. You and Mom really should've thought about keeping some details to yourself."

He smirks. "So, you're not pregnant. Why are you asking about when I found out I was a father?"

We smile and wave to Greta right before she slides into her car.

"You didn't want kids, right?" I ask.

"No."

"Yeah, that's what Mom said."

He puts his hand on my arm to stop me. "She said that? I meant no, you're wrong."

"Well—"

"I'd just opened Terra and Mare. Actually, I hadn't even served my first real table yet when your mom walked in holding you. I lived in the small apartment Dion lives in now. It wasn't that I didn't want kids. I just didn't think I was ready to have a kid at the time." He lightly taps my nose with the tip of his finger. "And I was wrong."

I smile and bat my eyelashes as if he couldn't resist my smile and charming personality when I was two years old.

"You were the apple of my eye." He winks, and we resume walking toward the bus stop.

"I guess what I mean is… things like that can change, right? Your mind?"

He laughs and stares down at me for a second. Although when I'm in heels I'm practically his height, I'm wearing my boots since I was only working at his office today. "If you only knew how many things I've changed my mind on over the course of my life. What does this have to do with specifically?"

I inhale a deep breath and the air flows back out in a stream of white mist. "Nothing specifically. I just wondered." I shrug.

His smile disappears. I know my dad, and he doesn't like that I'm being vague. He thought we were finally on our way to talking about the real issues in my life.

"I'm here when you need me." He repeats the same line he has since I returned home from UCLA seven years ago.

"I know. Thank you." A grateful smile crosses my lips as we continue walking.

We're almost at the bus stop when Marla Greene's black SUV breezes past us and parks in one of the few vacant spaces on the road. I must freeze because my dad wraps his arm around my shoulders and leads me toward the bus stop.

It's only Marla, I tell myself. I've seen her plenty and she never brings up Rylan to me. She's always polite enough to divert the topic to her million grandkids and how busy they keep her.

"Shit. I forgot, sweetie," my dad murmurs.

"It's okay."

It's not a big deal because I don't expect to see Rylan. After so many years, I know his drill—in and out of Sunrise Bay as fast as he can. Even if he was asked to be here to pick up some of the Greene kids, he would've declined because he wouldn't take the chance of seeing me.

We reach the bus stop and stand idly, waiting. The door of Marla's SUV opens, and it's clear that it's not Marla inside. As the person emerges, all the air in my lungs rushes out into a puff of white because Rylan Greene's face looks over the roof of his mom's SUV, his eyes finding me immediately.

"Should I kick his ass?" my dad whispers.

"What? Why?"

"Just wanted to offer in case…"

"No, Dad."

Rylan takes his jacket out of the back seat and puts it on. He never did like driving with his jacket on. Then he zips it up and walks over to us, trying to pocket the bulky keys that have every grandkid's school picture on the key chain, but he gives up trying after a bit.

"Mr. Bailey." He approaches with his hand out in front of him.

"Hi, Rylan. Here to get some of the kids?"

"Yeah." He rocks back on his heels. "Calista," he says softly to me.

A swift gust of wind travels my way from behind him and all I smell is his cologne. The same one I used to sample at stores to torture myself with because the scent always made the memories rush back.

"Hi," I manage to squeeze out.

Just then, Uncle Denver walks up and my dad starts to step away to say hello, but I tighten my grip on his arm. Dad stares down at me.

"What's up?" Uncle Denver asks, then spots Rylan and points at him. "Holy shit, it's Rylan Greene. The fucking center forward for Chicago." His tone is sarcastic because every time he sees Rylan, he says the same thing.

Thankfully, before any more awkwardness arises, the van pulls up. Instead of Ethel, Dori, and Midge inside with Earl at the helm, it's the other four residents I swear were secretly trained by them in the art of meddling.

Alice opens the door from the driver's seat. "We got your precious cargo."

Floyd gets out of the other side of the van, comes around, and waits with his hand extended as every kid home from college for the holidays comes down the van steps.

"Be careful, it's icy," he says.

My little sister Rhea smiles politely and thanks him as she was raised to do. Thankfully, she comes to me first and squeezes me tight.

"I cannot believe Rylan is, like, right there," she whispers, but when I take a chance and look at Rylan, I see she wasn't quiet enough. The red on his cheeks isn't just from the cold wind.

Emelia walks off the van without looking at anyone and gives Rylan a polite hello. Trey follows shortly after, and I hear the beep of Marla's SUV indicating that Rylan's unlocked it. I peek over again to see Rylan still standing there while his niece and nephew walk to the SUV.

Our eyes lock for a moment and I'm about to take the few steps to him to break the distance, but he speaks first.

"Have a Merry Christmas, Mr. Bailey and Mr. Bailey," he says to my dad and uncle.

They wave and wish him a Merry Christmas, telling him to wish his family well too.

"Merry Christmas, Calista," he says in a low voice, and the smallest smile graces his lips. Those kissable lips I loved so much. My name off his tongue sounds so good, and all I can think of is him thrusting inside me, whispering, "Calista, god, you feel amazing."

"Enjoy your time home," I say.

He nods before turning around and heading to the truck.

"Details," Rhea demands as she slides her arm through mine and tugs me away from the retirement home van.

Watching the rear lights of Rylan's vehicle should feel familiar to me. It's nothing new, but still, a pang of rage, jealousy, and resentment pierces my heart.

Chapter Four

JED

"Do you want me to go?" Molly asks when I finally read the family group text about the meeting at the family house tonight.

"No. I'll go."

"I could easily take Peyton, and Josh is old enough to stay by himself."

I hold up my phone. "Did you not see the text? No kids."

She rolls her eyes and sighs. "Nikki doesn't always put things very nicely. And knowing everyone, they won't pay attention to that anyway."

If Molly wasn't already attached to our family because she's Nikki's best friend, I'd be afraid she'd want to run away from me and my crazy family at some point.

"Come upstairs." I tug on her sweater and nod toward the staircase.

"I'm making dinner."

"Josh!" I yell.

No answer.

"He's playing video games with his friends. Leave him be."

She puts the spoon to my lips, and I do that dramatic thing with my tongue, running it along the edges of the spoon. It clearly doesn't make her hot and heavy like it does when roles are reversed. Hell, just the sight of Molly's tongue can still get my dick up.

"Mmm," I say. I'd say it even if the sauce sucked, but it doesn't.

Molly's on this kick where she wants a family recipe book to pass down to the kids. Every week she tries at least one new recipe with the hopes that everyone loves it and she can add it to the book. I truly don't understand it, but it's not my job to understand.

The front door opens, and the honk of a horn from the driveway tells us who is here.

"About time. She got off that plane forever ago." Molly drops the spoon and we both rush to the door.

When she sees us, Emelia drops her bags and smiles. "I'm home."

We suffocate her, hugging her from both sides, telling her how happy we are that she's home.

"Okay, guys." She pats our arms. "Guys." She does it again.

Josh walks downstairs and rounds the bottom of the staircase. "And they say they don't have favorites," he grumbles.

"We don't." Molly is the first to disengage, but I keep my arms around my baby girl.

I wanted her to go to college in Anchorage, but Molly insisted that Emelia needed to spread her wings. She spread them all right. Right into some cocky bastard's arms.

"Come in. I'm making a new recipe and I want your honest answer." Molly takes Emelia's hand and leads her to the kitchen. "And I can't wait to hear all about Dalton."

Emelia glances over her shoulder at me. I hope she missed the roll of my eyes.

"Is she here?" Peyton peeks around the corner at the top of the stairs. She's practically a mini-me of Emelia when she was six, other than her dark hair, which is like Molly's. I guess the Greene genes are strong.

"She is," I say.

Peyton rushes down the stairs in her plaid dress and stockings. She went shopping in downtown Anchorage today with Posey and her daughter, Keira. They saw Santa, had hot cocoa, and went to some doll store. Supposedly you have to dress up there, because usually my little Peyton is always in her stretchy clothes.

I hold my hands out for her, but she pushes past me and runs into the kitchen. "Emelia!"

She jumps, and in the small glimpse I get from the foyer down the hallway to the kitchen, Emelia catches her, and Peyton clings to her like a koala bear. "I missed you," she whispers.

I join them in the kitchen to find Emelia still holding Peyton, and I have to fight back fucking tears because my little girl is all grown up. With a douchebag for a boyfriend.

Molly holds up the spoon to Emelia. She sets Peyton on her feet then tastes it, nodding that it's good. Josh sits at the counter with a bag of chips that Molly takes away from him. He whines that he's starving, as he always does a half hour before dinner every night.

I soak up the feeling that my family is all under the same roof again. Molly turns on the radio, and Peyton begs Emelia to dance. Josh makes fun of them, and I smack him on the back of the head. Molly continues making dinner, so I help her with the garlic bread and make Josh prepare the lettuce. It feels like it used to when there were five of us living under this roof.

A half hour later, we're sitting at our small kitchen table, and I'm ecstatic to see the chair that's been vacant since August being occupied by its rightful owner.

"So, I've waited long enough. What's Dalton like?" Of course Molly has to broach this subject in front of me when I told her I didn't want Emelia to have a boyfriend her freshman year.

Emelia peeks at me as she twists her pasta with her fork. "Actually, you could see for yourself… he was thinking about coming up…"

"Wha—" A piece of noodle lodges in my throat. They all wait until I clear it out and take a sip of my water, which I really wish was scotch right now. "Alaska's a long way from Arizona."

Emelia tilts her head, and Molly pinches my leg under the table.

"That sounds nice. He could stay on the pullout in the den. When is he thinking of coming?"

I glare at Molly.

"For New Year's Eve. It would only be for a few days." Emelia keeps looking at me as though she fears I'm going to have a heart attack.

"Boy, you really don't value that place at the top of the Greene family tree under favorite, huh?" Josh says.

Emelia narrows her eyes at him in annoyance.

"We don't have favorites," Molly says.

"Except me," Peyton's cute voice pipes up. But one day she'll come home from college with a clown for a boyfriend too.

"Is it okay… if he comes to visit?" Emelia asks as my heart returns to its normal rhythm.

"Of course. Right, Jed? We'd love to meet him." Molly raises her eyebrows at me.

I hate when she does this. Because of this, we're all going to my parents' tonight. Molly needs to be punished.

I splash on my fakest smile, though I'm sure Emelia sees right through it. "Yeah. Can't wait."

I bury my head in my pasta, and the rest of the dinner is spent with Molly drilling Emelia about her classes, Peyton asking about the roommate we met when we moved Emelia in, and Josh asking how many football games she's been to.

After dinner, I put the dishes in the dishwasher while

Molly and Emelia clear the table. Then I get to washing the ones that can't go in the dishwasher, at least according to my wife. Personally, I don't see what the big deal is if the odd frying pan and pot make it into the damn thing.

Emelia grabs a drying towel and stands next to me. "I can dry."

She picks up the pot I just placed down on the towel I laid out. I look behind me and see that we're alone in the kitchen. Molly's done this a lot over the years when she thinks one of the kids and I need a minute of our own.

We do the dishes in silence for a few minutes until my brave girl broaches the subject once again.

"He reminds me a lot of you," she says softly.

A dark chuckle leaves my lips. "That's not a good thing. I'm fully aware of what an ass I am."

She giggles. "I wasn't looking for a relationship. I was taking your advice, but there was this one party, and my roommate drank too much. I was trying to get her back to our dorm, and I'd just gotten her out of the party, and she fell into the bushes. Dalton helped me get her to the dorm. The next day he'd transferred into my Psych 101 class. I don't know, Dad, it just felt like something more powerful than me was in control."

"Uh-huh," I mumble, although I understand what she's saying. When I finally noticed Molly, it didn't matter how much I fought it, I needed to be with her.

"He asked me out three times before I finally accepted a coffee date." She smiles at me and I shake my head.

"Should've made him wait until ten."

"Dad." She elbows my side.

I turn off the faucet and dry my hands with a paper towel. Pulling her into my chest, I kiss the top of her head. "Welcome home, kiddo. We missed you."

"And..."

"And I…" I blow out a breath. "I look forward to meeting him."

She squeezes me tightly around the middle. "Love you, Dad."

"Love you… so much." I close my eyes and a tear escapes. Clearing my throat and pulling away from her, I call to the rest of the household, "Get your coats. We're going over to Grandma and Grandpa's!"

Chapter Five

Mandi

Noah yawns, exhausted from all the holiday family shoots he's had this week. Last weekend, he also did pictures with Santa at the annual pancake breakfast the library puts on.

"I'm sorry." I rub his knee. "I suggested a Google doc and that we all just add our names and what we'll do."

He shrugs because he's used to my family by now. "Well, my parents can help out too."

I nod, glancing out the car window at the wreaths hung on each of the streetlights downtown. I've made my own list because I was always the one next to my mom when she did everything over the years. "I just know they're going to try to make me do it all. I can just hear them now, 'But Mandi already knows how to do everything.'"

"Don't let them steamroll you, baby." Noah turns down my parents' street.

"Grandma!" Maisie screams as we grow nearer.

"Remember, Grandma is sick, so you won't see her," I tell her.

"Then why are we here?" she asks.

"Well, Grandpa is here, and I'm sure all your cousins will be too. We need to get ready for Christmas!" The excitement in Noah's voice surprises me, and I give him a look that he clearly understands. "I think it's from having to feign excitement all week when I'm trying to get good shots from a bunch of grumpy toddlers."

"Don't turn too Saint Nick on me. I'd miss my grumpy guy."

He chuckles. "If this meeting takes more than an hour, your grumpy guy will be coming out."

"Mom?" Maisie says from the back seat.

I look at Noah. This has been the new thing lately—we're no longer Mommy and Daddy. We're Mom and Dad. Every time she says it, I wonder again why we decided on only one child. But we knew with all the travel, one would be easier to manage. Plus, she has so many cousins that it's like she has sibling relationships in her life anyway.

"Yeah, sweetie?"

Noah pulls into the driveway of my parents' house. We're the fifth car here, which means I can hopefully slide in as someone else is already taking charge. From Nikki's text message, I assume it might be her.

"Did you know Santa isn't real?" Maisie says matter-of-factly.

Noah slams on the brakes. "Sorry, the brakes are touchy." He slowly turns his head toward me, putting the truck in park while his eyeballs look as if they might pop out of his head.

"Yes, he is," I say without thinking, as though it was instinctual.

Noah's eyebrows rise again. We've never had a conversation on how to handle this situation, and regardless, I can't have her going in that house saying Santa isn't real.

Noah puts his arm out so his hand is resting on the back of my seat and he's looking back at our daughter. "What makes you say that?"

"Nina told me there's no way Santa would come to our small-town pancake breakfast. That he has more important things to do."

Noah bites his lip because damn Nina, she's way too smart for her own good.

"Listen, Mais, um…" For the first time in my parenting history, I have nothing. I don't want to ever lie to her, but this is Santa. I'd hoped to get one more Christmas with her believing in the big guy.

"He might not have been Santa, but he was Santa's helper." Noah smiles, obviously proud of himself for coming up with that.

"Why does he pretend to be Santa? Why can't he come in, like, a blue suit and go by his real name? Say who he really is?"

Noah eyes me like, *Where did this girl come from?* "She's eight, right?"

I chuckle. "Yep."

"We didn't skip, like, five years from our house to here?"

I laugh again. "Nope."

He turns his attention back to our daughter. "Because the kids want to see Santa, so they help him out."

"But—"

A knock on our window interrupts us, and Axel's mouth is pressed against the window, blowing out his cheeks. The boy must've gotten his whole "make everyone laugh" thing from Allie because Fisher has never been that way.

"Come on. We'll talk about this when we get home." I open my car door and round the back on autopilot so I can help Maisie get out.

Except she doesn't need my help. She's no longer in a car seat and can unbuckle and open the door herself. Where have I been? Of course she's questioning Santa Claus's authenticity. Why didn't I plan better for this?

"Axel!" Maisie yells, but I wrap my hand around her wrist to stop her. "Mom!"

God, I hate that word. "Mais, I need you to do something for me tonight."

"What?"

"Please don't mention anything about Santa Claus, okay? We'll talk about it at home tonight, but no need to rile the others up."

"They need to know if he's a fake," she whispers.

Noah's on the other side of the vehicle, asking Axel how eighth grade is and whether he's trying out for basketball.

"Just one night," I say and give her my best stern mother look in the hopes it will work.

"Fine. Can I go now?"

I release her, and she runs over to Axel.

He picks her up and spins her around before planting her back on her feet. "What's up, Maisie?"

"Is Santa real?" she asks him.

"Maisie!" Noah and I screech in unison while Axel looks at us with doe eyes.

Maisie shrugs. "What? He'll tell me the truth."

My breath lodges in my throat as we wait for him to answer.

"Of course he is," Axel says.

Noah puts his arm around me, squeezing my shoulder.

"Okay." Maisie walks into the house with Axel, and I pray that's the end of the conversation for tonight.

"It hurts a little that she so easily believes Axel over us," Noah says on our way into the house from the garage.

"When did we become the bad guys who lie?" I whisper.

"When we became Mom and Dad instead of Mommy and Daddy." My lower lip sticks out, and Noah wraps me in his arms. "Oh sweetie, it's not too late. We can have another one."

I push his chest. "We're ten years away from an empty house."

He laughs. "There's my girl." Then he leans in and kisses my forehead.

I have no idea how Mom is supposed to be resting

upstairs with the party-like atmosphere inside the house. But that's my family. We're like a roaming party.

We dodge Shay as she goes into the laundry room—probably looking for a drink—but a pissed-off Posey is right behind her, talking through a clenched jaw. She spots us and puts on a fake smile.

When we overhear Posey yelling at Shay about her attitude and the rolling of her eyes, Noah mumbles, "I'm not looking forward to those years."

Once we reach the family room, all the adults are sitting on the furniture or the floor, discussing the various duties to be done. Actually, most of them are making excuses as to why they can't do a certain job. I look over at Noah and he shakes his head.

"Stay strong," he whispers in my ear.

Nikki's son Little Noah walks by, and my Noah takes him in a headlock, giving him a noogie.

"So, we meet again, Little Noah," my Noah says.

"Oh, fuck," Little Noah says.

The room silences and my Noah releases him. It's a game they've played for years, but Little Noah just swore.

Nikki gets up from the couch and walks over to her son. "What did you just say?"

Logan's quick to come to his wife's aid. I slide between them and join the rest of the family watching. But Nikki grabs Little Noah by the arm and escorts him out of the room with Logan following.

"Way to get him in trouble," Cade says to Noah jokingly.

I look around the room, making sure there aren't any young ears around. "Just a precaution, heads-up that our little one is questioning Santa."

Groans ring through the group because we all know what that means. Each time one of the kids stops believing, it threatens the younger kids' belief in Santa as well.

"She's so young," Presley says.

I nod.

"She's Mandi's, so…" Jed shrugs.

I scowl at him. "What does that mean?"

"You've always been the one who analyzes everything. Of course those genes slipped through."

"You make it sound like a bad thing?" I raise an eyebrow.

"Stop it, both of you. Let's get these tasks handled." Hank puts his arms out to each of us as if we're about to spar or something. Then he hands me a piece of paper. "What'd you think?"

I accept it because he's Hank, and he's in over his head on this one. I read the list and pick up a pencil from the table. I randomly write people's names on each of the items and hand it back. "We're all capable of doing the jobs, so I don't want to hear any complaints."

Everyone scrambles to get a look at what I've assigned them, then there are a bunch of grumbles and shitty looks thrown my way. If they don't like it, then they should've taken charge themselves.

CADE

I walk down the candy aisle with Presley. We left Leighton in charge of her sister and brother because they can't see that what we're buying is what they'll find in their stockings on Christmas morning.

"How did we get stuck with stocking stuffers?" I follow Presley.

"Why are you complaining? This is easy. We'll get some candy, then I'll go get some small stuff to fill in the gaps." She stops and looks over the labels of some of the candy.

Candy is candy. You're not going to find vitamins in one versus the other.

"Why does Marla even give the kids a stocking? That's the parents' responsibility."

She huffs and drops both candy bags, turning around to face me. This isn't good. My wife can be scary when she's upset. Like the time I off-handily mentioned Micah, our youngest, was an oops. I'll never forget that look. But he was. He came six years after his sister. Eventually the kid will figure it out.

"Why are you being such a pest about this?" Presley asks.

I huff and stand there idly until I can form the words correctly. My wife, being all too familiar with me, waits patiently, holding the basket.

"How come Adam got to chop down a tree? Is it because

I'm old?" I look down at myself. Sure, I'm not the superfit guy I was when I married Presley, but I'm not out of shape either.

Her perfectly shaped eyebrows arch. "Seriously? Your ego is bruised because you were put on stocking duty?"

"Well, Jed is doing the lights." Jesus, even I can hear the whine in my voice.

She thinks for a moment because Presley is a problem solver. Especially when it comes to my or the kids' happiness.

"I'm sure one of them would be happy to trade." She plucks my phone out of my hand and holds it up. "Call one of them."

I take the phone from her. "Maybe I will."

"Tell me before I buy all this stuff." She holds up the basket.

It's now or never. She waits, eyeing the phone in my hand.

Crap, maybe I am acting like a baby, but shit, I'm fucking forty-nine years old. I'll be fifty next year, and although I love my life, I don't wanna grow old. Back in the day, Jed and I would've gotten the hardest jobs because we were the oldest and the strongest.

"Well?" Presley is baiting me because she knows how stupid I'm being.

I pocket my cell phone. "I'm not going to change anything."

She smiles. "Smart man. Now let's finish this because we have a busy week. Micah's Christmas show at Northern Lights is coming up, Morgan is hosting some Christmas exchange with her friends, and Leighton wants to go sledding with her friends. Plus, we have all our own family traditions to handle as well."

I help her pick out the candy, thankful now that I don't have to worry about finding the perfect tree or hanging up lights. Truthfully, Jed wouldn't even have a job had our parents found time to put up the lights sooner. But Hank and

Marla went on a vacation after Thanksgiving, and I think time kept slipping away from them. It's not very Marla-like, truthfully. It makes me wonder if they're getting tired of running the Christmas show every year.

"Do you think Marla and Dad are getting too old to host?" I ask at the checkout while Presley's dumping all the candy on the counter.

The cashier scans each item, not paying us much attention.

"Please tell me I'll handle fifty better than you are." Presley smiles at the cashier. The kid couldn't care less.

She pays, and I grab the bags, following her out to the truck.

Once we're secure and it's only us, she faces me. "I hate to be the one to tell you this, but one day you're going to die." My shoulders slouch, and she laughs. "I'm sorry. I hate to be the one to break it to you."

I shake my head and start the truck. "Seat belt."

She straps herself in. "I know fifty is hard. I'll be right there with you. But you're still my big, strong, gorgeous husband."

"I need to start running again."

She unclicks her seat belt.

"We need to get home." I eye the seat belt as she releases it.

"We have time. Leighton can watch her siblings." She moves over the center console, straddling my lap and unclicking my seat belt in the process.

"Damn, baby." It feels like a lifetime since we've done anything like this. "Thank God for tinted windows."

She leans back on the steering wheel, unbuckling my belt and opening my jeans, all while her eyes promise what we're about to do.

"We have a bed at home," I say—for what reason, I have no idea. At the same time I say it, I tilt the seat back to give her more room.

"I'm not looking for a bed," she whispers, taking my dick out of my boxer briefs.

She runs her hand up and down my shaft, and fuck, I'm back to when we first started dating. The way neither of us could keep our hands off one another. My hands fiddle with the hem of her T-shirt and, inch by inch, move up her torso until both hands cup her tits that are covered in a bra with too much fucking padding. I tug the cups down and her back arches, offering me her breasts. All I want to do is feast on them.

"Come closer, baby," I whisper.

She slides up on me, her leggings running along my length. They're buttery soft.

Lifting her shirt, I take one nipple into my mouth, and she moans, her fingers fiddling with my hair that's not nearly the length it was when we first started dating. It's shorter now, respectable for a father of three and a businessman within the community. I'm no longer the shaggy kid with a start-up bar and grill.

"More," she pleads and the hell if I'm going to tell her no. "I need you inside me, Cade. Now."

My mouth reluctantly comes off her tit while she gets my pants down to my ankles. Her shoes fly to the back of the truck, and her leggings and panties disappear with them.

Then my dick rubs along her wetness and fuck, I can barely take it. She guides me inside her.

Long gone are the times of worrying about condoms. After Micah, I had a vasectomy. No more surprises for us.

She sinks down onto me, and my hands move to her hips. "Damn, you feel so good."

"So do you." She slides up and back down, her hands on my shoulders to steady herself. "I feel like it's been months."

"Me too. We really need to plan date nights. *Hotel* date nights."

"Yeah," she groans. "I mean, we have a huge-ass family.

How come we don't take advantage of all the built-in babysitters?"

My hands grab her hips, pulling up and slamming her down on me. "Because we're morons. Fuck, honey, I'm gonna lose it soon."

Her breathing becomes more labored, and I pick up my hips from the seat while slamming her onto me to get as deep as I can. The truck grows hot and humid inside and sweat beads my forehead.

"I love you," she says before her lips smash against mine.

And this is just one of the things I love about my wife—she's secure within herself. She takes what she wants from me because she knows I'll give it all when it comes to her.

"I'm close. Play with my clit."

I keep one hand on her hip and move the other to her clit. Her back arches, resting on the steering wheel as my thumb rubs circles and I keep a hectic pace moving in and out of her.

"Cade!" she shouts.

I don't slow my pace until the walls of her pussy contract around my cock. That's all I need for my orgasm to come right after. One last push and I lock myself inside her, pumping my release.

Somewhere between my orgasm and her falling forward into my arms, the truck starts rolling.

"Shit." I search everywhere for the reason, but it's hard since Presley is sitting on me.

My foot gets caught in my pants and I hit the gas pedal, slamming us into one of the handicapped sign poles for the parking spots in front of us.

Presley laughs, and her long blonde hair falls on me. "We're going to be the latest rumor."

I laugh with my wife and run my hand up and down her back. "I don't care. Shows we aren't too old to fuck in a truck."

She looks up at me and kisses my jaw. "It was hot and all, but I kind of like all the room we have on our bed."

I shake my head, chuckling, because I agree. There are about a million other things I wanted to do to her that I couldn't. "And it would've been nice to save the car insurance deductible for Christmas presents."

"True."

We both laugh, and I'm reminded exactly why I fell in love with this woman in the first place.

Chapter Seven

Posey

Why did I get stuck with the gingerbread houses? I'm not a baker. This is totally a Mandi and Noah thing. But since I am on gingerbread duty, I figured it would be nice for the girls and me to do it together. I went to the store early this morning to get all the supplies for my mom's recipe. I remember making these with my mom every year, and it's a special time between mother and daughter.

Sometimes I think our family is so big that we lose sight of all the holiday traditions that were kept in our smaller families before they were blended. Now Mom and Hank make the gingerbread and have the houses assembled before all of us get there. Each family has its own to decorate as they wish.

"Shay!" I call when I walk through the back door into the kitchen. Gavin is still working until Christmas Eve because, as he puts it, the senator doesn't get a holiday vacation. It's not like there's a ton going on.

Kiera prances into the kitchen from the family room in her pajamas, her red hair a tangled mess. No doubt she watched YouTube the entire time I was away. "Are we making gingerbread houses?" she asks, sliding up on a breakfast bar chair.

I lower the bags onto the counter. "We sure are."

"Mommy?" she asks in that inquisitive voice as she so often does now.

I forgot how many questions Shay used to ask at the same age. Wanting to know how everything works and why things are a certain way.

I tighten my hands on the molasses bottle because after Maisie's questions last night, I fear my Kiera isn't going to believe in Santa soon either.

"Yeah?" I purposely turn away from her just in case my face will give it away. Between the way Shay and I can't stop being at each other's throats, if Kiera no longer believes in Santa, I might have a mental breakdown.

"You don't bake."

Relief floods me, and all the tension flows from my body. "I know. I was meant to do hair."

"Speaking of which, you cut too much off last weekend." Shay comes in, brushing her red hair that has more of an auburn look, thanks to her dad's darker tones.

"I took off the dead ends, and if you would stop using so much heat on it on a daily basis, the ends wouldn't get that bad so fast."

"Okay, Mom." She goes into the fridge and grabs a yogurt. "I'll be the laughingstock of the school if I'm wearing my hair like Kiera."

"What's wrong with my hair?" Kiera touches her hair.

"Nothing, it's beautiful," I say.

"To a bird," Shay says.

"Mommy, will you brush it and put it in braids today?" Kiera says with a slight tinge of sadness as though she's one second from crying. She looks up to her big sister. I wish Shay could see that and be nice to her.

"Sure. Let's just get these groceries unpacked and then we'll get ready."

"I'm going over to Naomi's today," Shay says. "Her mom said she'd take us to Anchorage to shop. Can I have some money?"

Again, tension racks my body because it's only nine in the morning and we're going to have our first argument of the day. "We're going to make gingerbread houses, remember?"

"Can't we do it tonight?"

"We have to make eleven, and I was going to do thirteen just in case something happened to some of them."

"Thirteen is an unlucky number," Shay says, her phone an inch away from her face.

"Where'd you hear that?"

She rolls her eyes and mumbles something about joining this century.

I'm sure she saw it on that damn app. As if all holy knowledge can be found on her phone. She'd trust a stranger on that thing more than me, I think.

"Then I'll make fourteen. All the more reason why I need you here. Can't you and Naomi plan it for another day?" I take out the butter and eggs to get them to room temperature while I get Kiera ready to start the day.

"Her mom has to work later."

"And so do I. I took this morning and early afternoon off. During Christmas."

Any other time of year, I'd usually have the entire day off, but at the holidays, everyone wants their hair done. In years past, I've worked all the way through to Christmas, and usually later hours than normal, but lately I feel as though I'm losing my connection with Shay, and I thought that maybe we could bond while she was out of school. Guess I was wrong.

She huffs. "Fine. I'll tell Naomi I can't go." She takes her phone and walks out of the room.

"Mommy? Hair?" Kiera comes down with a brush and her ponytail holders.

"Give me one second." I swipe my phone and hit Gavin's name to call him, heading to another room quickly before I say something I'll regret in front of my daughter.

Gavin picks up right away. "How are the gingerbread houses going?"

"I haven't made them. It's only nine."

"Uh-oh, what's wrong? I hear it in your voice."

"She's so unreasonable, Gavin."

I know he's tired of Shay's attitude and the way she keeps pushing every boundary we've set too. I tell him about Naomi and the mall. I'm just venting because he's the only one who understands.

"Just be firm with her."

"And have her pissed off the whole day? I already don't want to spend my day doing this with her when she's being all… anyway, I think I'm just going to let her go."

"You can't give in like that, Posey."

"Then you come home and deal with it." I hang up and send Gavin an apology text right after. When will my house be back to normal?

I head into the kitchen and see Kiera in the family room, watching YouTube. Oh, how I miss when Shay was that age.

"Shay!" I shout.

She comes down the stairs in a pair of sweatpants and a baggy shirt, throwing herself into a chair. "How long is this going to take?"

I dig into my purse and grab some money. "Here. Have fun with Naomi."

Her eyes light up, and she accepts the money. "Thanks, Mom." She gives me a one-arm kind of hug that I don't really return. I'm still mad. "I have to go change."

She's gone again, upstairs to her room where she spends the majority of her time these days.

I go to the family room and Kiera sits down between my legs, allowing me to brush and braid her hair. As she's entranced in some show, I can't help but think how fast it all goes. Shay was just like Kiera once, wanting to come to the shop with me and sweep up hair between clients. She'd refill the candy jar and stack the magazines.

I can't help but feel like she's gone. I've lost her already.

I finish Kiera's braids and she starts changing out of her pajamas and into the outfit I took out for her today. She's not shy, which I realize I'll have to address soon.

I go into the kitchen and grab the recipe to read it over, my mom's handwriting so familiar to me. Memories flood my mind—me laughing with my sisters as we made the gingerbread houses. When Chevelle joined our family, her first time joining in, she had the biggest smile the entire time. This is a family tradition, I tell myself.

"Oh, screw it." I put down the recipe and walk up the stairs.

I knock on Shay's door and wait for her to tell me I can come in. She's putting on mascara at her mirror while talking with Naomi about what they're going to get while they're at the mall. I sit on the edge of her bed and wait.

Shay eventually gets the hint and hangs up. "What's up?"

"I'm sorry, Shay, but you're going to stay home and make the gingerbread houses with us today."

"What?" Her mascara drops from her hand onto her vanity. "Why?"

I stand, knowing this conversation will be short and maybe this year won't be the best memory of making gingerbread houses, but so be it. "Because it's a tradition. One I should've initiated a long time ago. You can be mean and sulk the entire day while we're doing it, but you're going to do it. Now, I hope you'll try to enjoy your time with us, but how you react is completely up to you. You choose whether to make this an enjoyable day or an unbearable one."

I walk out of her room and head back down the stairs.

I swoop up Kiera. "Ready?"

"Yep."

I grab our three aprons from the closet and I'm putting on

Kiera's when Shay comes downstairs, her hair pulled back in a ponytail. Kiera and I stare at her for a beat.

"Can I have my apron?" Shay asks nicely, and I smile, handing it over.

I'm not expecting immediate results, but I'll take a half smile and politeness any day of the week.

Chapter Eight

RYLAN

Mom's still in bed and I'm stuck figuring out the menu with Dad. We're going to have to give everyone a dish to prepare. That's the only way to pull this off. My mom was always a little more frazzled during the holidays, running around and preparing items to cross off her list, which I never understood, but I do now. I mean, did she even enjoy the holidays?

I'm on my way to buy luminaries and poinsettias for our front porch and driveway. I could easily buy both of those items downtown in Sunrise Bay, but it's as though my mom's SUV has a mind of its own because I'm driving toward Lake Starlight.

Who am I kidding? I know exactly why I'm going to Lake Starlight. I'm like an addict who needs a fix. One I've convinced myself will tide me over until I can be in her presence again the next time I visit.

I switch my mom's Christmas music to any other station, finding "One" by U2 on the next one and leaving it there.

When I reach Lake Starlight, I park along the street by the florist and look around as though maybe Calista knows I am coming and will magically appear. I only know where she lives because I looked it up. Stalked her like some creep who's no longer invited to know anything about her life, which is pretty on point.

After getting out of the SUV, I walk into the florist shop.

A girl leans out from behind a big bouquet of flowers. "Rylan Greene?"

I peek around the huge assortment. I know which Baileys are her parents, but I'm not sure which sister this is.

"Maven," she says.

I nod and smile. "Hey, how are you?"

She shrugs. "It's just a part-time job. I'm a senior in high school now. What do you need?"

"Um…"

One thing I've always loved about Calista is her relationship with her cousins. Each one is unique. They'd call at the worst times, and she'd always answer and listen to them. Okay, back then, sometimes I was annoyed as fuck, especially when we were in bed. But now with some distance, I can see that it's special.

"Flowers? Plants?" Maven's staring at me as though I'm crazy, which I probably look because I want to run down the streets of Lake Starlight screaming Calista's name.

God, get a fucking grip, man.

"Poinsettias?" I ask as though she would have no idea what the most popular holiday plant is.

"Oh yeah. We just got another shipment in. Northern Lights took them all last week, and we had to scramble." She rounds the counter. "Then again, you could've found some by you in Sunrise Bay." She raises her eyebrows for a second before showing me the big display.

"They were sold out."

"Oh."

She probably knows I'm lying, but I have no good excuse to be here, to want to be near Calista after the end of us. It was hard enough the last time we said goodbye.

"I'll take six. Can I borrow this cart?"

"Yeah, no problem."

I pull the cart over and put the six poinsettias on it.

"I'll ring you up when you're ready. Is there anything else I can help you with?" She has a lilt to her voice that says she thinks I should. Is she insinuating I send something to Calista?

"I'm okay, thanks though."

"All right." She walks away, and I hear her fingers on the cash register, pressing hard.

Pushing the cart over to the counter, I pull out my wallet and spot the flowers to my right. "Are those…"

"Camellias? Yes. We just got them in. Blush pink with white tips. They're a lot of people's favorites…"

I guess I'm not the only person who knows Calista's favorite flower.

I admire the camellias, remembering my conversation with Calista once after a fight when I'd sent her a bouquet of flowers, and she gushed about the camellias. She'd scoured the internet to find their name. Every bouquet I gave or sent to her after that was only camellias, and each time, she'd say how they made her smile.

Then the memory of seeing her days ago at the bus stop comes to mind. How she wasn't smiling. Her smile can light up the worst of days. Take you from a shitty mood to making you feel as though your heart might explode. She should always be smiling.

"I'll take a dozen and I'd like them sent to—"

Maven waves me off. "Oh, no worries, I know where they go." She slides a card in front of me. "Just fill this out, and I promise not to read it." She chuckles, which makes me think she probably will.

I blow out a breath. She tells me the total and I hand over my credit card. "Thanks." I sign and return my attention to the card. Deciding on something simple that tells her what I hope for her, I jot it down and seal the envelope.

"Our delivery person is already out on a delivery, but as soon as he gets back, I'll have him run them over."

"Thanks." I stand there, unsure what to do now. "I've got to go find luminaries, so… merry Christmas, Maven."

"Merry Christmas," she says. "And thank you for your purchase. Do you need—"

"No, I've got it."

I walk out the door, pushing the cart, and put all the poinsettias in the back of my mom's SUV. I return the cart and walk down to the hardware store, hoping they have what I need. I know my mom usually gets the luminaries from George at Handyman Haven in Sunrise Bay.

Thankfully, they're right there by the Christmas stuff and I pick up three packs since my mom likes to use them to line the driveway. When I check out, the guy behind the counter—his name tag says Jack—looks me over after accepting my card.

He runs it and reads the name again, handing it back to me. "I thought that was you. Heck of a season."

I put the card back in my wallet. "Thanks."

"What brings you here? George a little too nosy?" He laughs.

"Ah," I say and push my hand through my hair. "Just needed a change of scenery."

"I get that. Although I don't leave Lake Starlight too often." He packages my luminaries. "I help coach the high school baseball team with Austin Bailey."

Does everyone know a damn Bailey in this town?

"Oh nice."

"And you were coached by Jamie Ferguson, right? Sedona Bailey's husband."

"Yeah." I'm starting to realize that coming to Lake Starlight was a very bad idea.

"Good luck next season. Not that you need it."

I shake his hand. "Thank you."

With the bag in my hand, I walk out of the hardware store.

Somehow the cold seems extra bitter today. Or maybe living in the lower forty-eight has made me soft.

Pressing my luck, I stop at Lard Have Mercy and grab a pie. There can never be too many desserts. Then I stop at Brewed Awakenings to get a coffee with the hopes it will help me feel better. On my way back to the car, someone calls my name.

"Rylan!"

I turn to see Calista standing in the doorframe of not where I thought her apartment was. She's at the bottom of a staircase with her coat half on and slippers on her feet. It looks as if she came from the apartment above her dad's restaurant, Terra and Mare.

I walk over, biting my lip to stop from smiling because this is what I'd hoped for when I drove down here. This is the outcome I wanted. And she looks so good with her hair in a messy bun, joggers, and a T-shirt that cuts off at her navel. Don't get me wrong, she's hot in anything she wears.

"Hey."

"Follow me." She walks up the stairs into the apartment and I follow, hoping like hell my flowers were the olive branch and we're actually going to have a real conversation.

Once we're in the apartment, she doesn't shut the door. Instead, she picks up the vase of flowers and tries to hand them to me. "Here you go. Give them to someone else."

I set everything in my hands on the table near the door and stuff my hands in my pockets. "No."

She cocks her head and juts out her hip. "This isn't funny. Why would you send me flowers?" Her voice is louder than normal.

"Where are we?" I spot a game console which doesn't scream Calista. I mean, she would occasionally play with me, but it wasn't really something she did on her own. Not to mention the sink full of dishes and discarded shirts and sweatshirts.

"Dion's. Never mind where we are. You need to take these back."

I take my chances and step forward. "Why?" I lower my voice.

"Don't even try it, Ry. We're over, remember?"

"I know, and I sent those to you because I was at the florist, and I saw them and remembered you love them and that they make you smile. You weren't smiling the other day when I saw you, and you should be smiling every fucking day." I step closer and she holds the vase out to keep me back.

"They aren't my favorite anymore."

"Lie."

"Maybe my love for these flowers died along with…"

I inhale deeply and our eyes lock, testing one another. I wait a second for her to finish that sentence because we both know that what we had, what we felt for one another will never go away, not totally.

"Put the flowers down," I say.

"You're not the boss of me. Take them or I drop them and they die a slow, wilted death."

"Calista." I take the vase from her hands and lean closer to her, placing them on the counter.

For a moment, we stand there, inhaling one another's scent. The closeness is so familiar. Maybe it's the competitive athlete in me or the fact that I've always gone after what I wanted in life, but right now, I want to taste her, savor her, remember her. Every day since she walked out, the remembrance of having her has grown dimmer and I want a refresher.

My hand lands on her hip and I step into her, locking her against the counter with my hips while my lips capture hers. And holy hell, it's as intoxicating as always. Maybe even more so, because now I know what it's like to live without her.

Chapter Nine

ADAM

We decide to go as a family to cut down the tree, my responsibility on the Greene family to-do list.

"I think we should buy your parents an artificial one. They're getting too old to be coming out here and cutting down their own tree," Lucy says as we trudge through the snow.

Although Lucy does a lot with me outdoors, this isn't really her thing. She definitely enjoys when the weather is warmer.

"They'll never hear of it."

Althea groans.

Lucy laughs and the two of them stay back a few steps, talking about some new boy that Althea likes. Let's just say I'm not doing well being the dad of a thirteen-year-old girl. My daughter seems a little boy crazy if you ask me. It's worse when I think about how she's only one year off from when Lucy and I became stuck like glue throughout high school.

"You've been quiet since you've been back?" I say to Trey on my right.

He shrugs. "We've all been busy with Grandma being sick."

"School is going well? We're not in for a surprise this semester?"

Trey usually only grows quiet when he feels as though

he's disappointed us. And since he's on a partial scholarship for his academics, if his grades slip, Lucy and I would have to find a way to keep him in college. On a forest ranger and a teacher's salary, that would be hard.

"Yeah, I'm good there. My adviser says I'm on track to graduate and told me if I'm thinking about graduate or law or medical school, now is the time to get those ducks in a row."

"And are you?"

He shrugs again. "Right now, I can't imagine being in school for that much longer. I enjoy it but I'm anxious to actually *do something, you* know?"

I laugh. "I barely made it through ranger training, so I understand you there. Talk to your mother who did the full four years."

He glances back and nods, looking a little apprehensive.

I squeeze his shoulder. Trey is adopted, so we don't look alike. He's shorter than me, with blond hair and blue eyes—the opposite of both his mother and me—but I never think about those differences. He's just Trey, my son. "Deciding on your future can be hard. I'm happy to sit down and talk it out. I'm sure your mom would be too."

He nods a couple times. "Thanks, Dad."

I tell ya, there's nothing better than hearing that word.

"That's a good one!" Althea points, and we all look to see a tree that would work.

"It is," I say.

We all walk over to it, and Trey hands me the saw. We always cut down our tree ourselves and I've always been the one to saw it down.

"You do it," I tell him.

"Really?" Trey says like an excited twelve-year-old.

"Definitely. I'm getting old."

Trey lies down in the snow while I hold the trunk, then I pass him the saw.

"Speaking of getting old, Presley told me Cade took the news hard about you getting to cut down the tree," Lucy says.

"What?"

"He does have gray hair," Althea says. "And aren't you guys planning some trip with just the parents for him and Uncle Jed's fiftieth?"

I glance at Lucy. Althea overhears everything.

"Fifty isn't old," I say.

"He acts like we're treating him like he's Ethel by not giving him the job of cutting down the tree." Lucy shakes her head.

"Not to mention, everyone knows we go every year to cut down our own tree. It's not a big deal." But I've known for some time that Cade is struggling with growing older.

"Whatever, let's just get this cut and get it over to your parents." Lucy runs her hands up and down her arms.

Trey does a great job of cutting down the tree, and we get it in the bed of my truck, tying it down just in case.

"You make a great partner," I say. "I should've had you help me before."

"I wasn't all that interested."

Which is true. Trey is more intellectual, doesn't care for the outdoors very much. Reads books on the government and politics for fun. I always enjoy when we find something we can do together.

When we get to Dad and Marla's, Rylan is just pulling up. His hair looks a little messed up, and he's got a pissed-off expression.

"Hey, Ryguy." I go to the back of my truck.

"Ah, the tree cutters." He takes the poinsettias out of Marla's SUV and brings them to the front of the house.

"Thea, go help Uncle Rylan," I tell her.

She skips over and takes a poinsettia.

"Thanks," he says.

"When was your first girlfriend?" she asks him.

For some reason, I don't think now is the time to ask, especially since the bag he's holding says Hammer Time - Lake Starlight, Alaska. "Later, Thea."

Rylan catches me reading the bag and says, "George was out."

I nod and hold up my hands as though it's none of my business.

Trey gets on one side and I get on the other of the tree, and we walk it up to the closed garage. I need to find my dad's tree base.

"Hank? Marla?" Lucy walks into the house through the garage door and we all follow.

Althea continues to tell Rylan that I don't really want her to have a boyfriend, but it's hypocritical because of how Lucy and I fell in love so young.

"Love is complicated, Thea. Give yourself some time, there's no rush. When he comes into your life, you'll know the time is right."

She looks at Rylan, clearly perplexed.

We find my dad putting up garland on the stair railing while Marla is trying to direct him from bed.

"Do you hear me, Hank? Every other rung!"

My dad rolls his eyes and gives us a look.

"Can we go see Grandma?" Althea asks.

"Hi, babies! Oh, how I miss you," Marla calls down the stairs.

"Afraid she's still got a fever. But she's coming into her own again. Believe me," my dad says.

"How does it look, Lucy? Good?" Marla hollers down, and I shake my head.

"Great. It looks great." Lucy gives my dad a thumbs-up.

"I'm starving," Rylan says and disappears into the kitchen.

"Want help, Grandpa?" Trey asks and takes a piece of garland.

"I can help too," Althea says, taking another piece.

"You two are lifesavers." Dad smiles over at us.

"I got the tree." I thumb outside.

"Lucy, come talk to me from the upstairs hallway," Marla says, and Lucy happily obliges.

"You do know I'm a teacher, so I could probably come in there and not get sick?" my wife says.

"Just stay out there to be safe."

My dad and I go outside and get the tree while Trey and Althea work on the garland. I'm trimming some of the smaller branches off the base of the trunk when a man starts up the driveway. My dad meets him halfway and doesn't seem to know who he is. They shake hands and my dad looks back at me. Something about the entire scene has my insides in knots. Then my dad and the man walk up to me. I kill the chainsaw engine and take off my protective glasses.

"Adam," my dad says.

I've only seen my dad at a loss for how to approach a subject a few times in my life, and the one I remember most is when he had to sit us down and tell us our mother was dead and wasn't coming back.

I put out my hand. "I'm Adam Greene."

The man nods. "I know. My name is Hugh McGowen."

I step back and panic flares in his eyes. Trey's last name before he was adopted was McGowen.

He holds up his hands. "I'm not here to cause trouble."

My entire being goes into protective mode. Lucy, Althea, Trey. Hugh McGowen is a threat to our family. Is this why Trey has been so quiet lately?

"I was incarcerated when Trey was born. In and out of jail. His mom was no better for him. The best thing we did was sign over our rights so he could be adopted by a family like yours."

My stomach turns over. "How did you find us?"

Hugh looks a little sheepish. "I did some asking around.

Seems you Greenes are well known around here. Didn't take much to find out that if you weren't at home, you might be here." He holds his hands up in front of him. "Don't worry, I didn't tell anyone who I was or why I was here."

"I called the agency." Trey stands at the garage opening, staring at his biological father. "I'm over eighteen. I inquired."

I turn to face him. "Is this why you've been quiet?"

"I don't want you or Mom to be upset."

"You can talk to us about this. Why go behind our backs?" I shake my head, unable to believe he didn't think he could come to us with this.

"I just wanted to know where I came from. I figured he wouldn't want anything to do with me anyway."

"I've waited and hoped you'd come find me someday," Hugh says.

"Why don't we all go in and talk about this over coffee?" my dad suggests.

Trey won't stop looking at me as though he fears he's done something wrong. We can have coffee, but I walk over to my son and wrap my arms around him, holding him tightly.

He breaks down in tears. "I didn't think he'd want anything to do with me. I thought I'd just see for myself and tell him how I feel. I never thought he'd come here. I'm so sorry, Dad." He sobs into my neck.

"Don't apologize for anything. Your mom and I always knew you and Thea might be curious. And that's okay. We should've told you that a long time ago." My own tears escape, and I pull back to look him in the eyes. "Let's all go inside and get to know one another, okay?"

Trey nods, a slight smile forming, but the best thing is that the tension I've noticed laced through his body since his return disappears.

XAVIER

"What the f—"

"Careful now," Clara warns.

"I swore we raised them a helluva lot better than this." I grab Sam's arm and bring him by my side, whispering, "Calm down or you're going to the car."

The kid gives me a look that says he'd like to see me try. He's always toeing the line. Who wanted all these kids anyway?

"You did." Clara answers the question I asked in my head because my wife has known me my entire life and always seems to know what I'm thinking.

"Let's face it, you getting pregnant with twins was—"

"What, Dad?" Isaiah asks.

Clara stares at me with a smirk.

"A blessing." I run my hand through my son's dark hair. "You guys are a blessing."

He smiles and runs right toward the scooters and the bikes.

Sure as shit, Sam hops on a scooter and rides it down the aisles.

"Out of four, we couldn't get one girl?" I whine to Clara, taking her hand.

"I told you we could've ordered all this online, but you

said it didn't have the same effect." She steps into me and kisses my cheek.

"You know how I feel."

I watch our four boys, all way too spoiled for their own good. My only saving grace is raising them in my hometown, but even in Sunrise Bay, some people put my kids on some pedestal because of what I accomplished in professional football. Clara and I toyed with moving somewhere people wouldn't know us, but someone would figure it out eventually and word would spread anyway.

"Then you have to endure this outing. Besides, there's hardly anyone here."

She's right, she picked the right time to be here. It's first thing in the morning and the toy store is pretty much empty.

"This was a bad idea." I gesture to the boys. "Look at them. I'm gonna end up on some gossip site about how my kids are out of control."

She laughs. "Sweetie, we're not worth gossiping about anymore."

I walk down the aisle with my wife as our kids whiz by us on different equipment that shouldn't be ridden in the store. She's right. No one gives a shit about my life anymore. At least not anyone in journalism. And it's been heaven. But there are still some forever fans, overzealous enough to report me to some online blog or another.

I smack my wife's ass. "Thank God. I always had to worry about someone stealing you away from me."

She stares blankly, shakes her head, and claps her hands. "Let's go, boys, time to pick out the gifts." She pulls the slips of paper she got from the underprivileged youth charity out of her purse.

The boys line up around her, ready for their jobs, and watching them makes me wonder how she got all the respect around our house. Even after I retired, I did some commentating for a while, unable to hang up my career for good. Clara's been holding down the fort all this time. I'm thankful that my kids are still so young. Our oldest is only eight years old, so there's still lots of time for me to be a daily presence in their lives.

"Dad, you're still gonna coach me next year, right?" Jaden, our oldest, asks as we pass by the footballs on the shelf. "All the other dads were super excited after this season."

"Yeah, we'll figure it out."

The other dads are excited because they think I can make their kid a star athlete. That maybe their boy will be the next big player to come out of Sunrise Bay. But Fisher and Jed coached their son's team to the youth Super Bowl for our area and won. Neither of them went pro. Having me as a coach doesn't necessarily ensure success.

When I was asked to coach, I told Clara that I was scared. Scared to ruin our kids' love of a game. What if I'm one of those parents who scream and yell at my kids for not playing perfectly? I'd never forgive myself. She told me she'd never allow that to happen, which I know is true. She always keeps me in check.

"What about me? Will you coach me? It'll be mine and Isaiah's first year." Sam looks up at me with wide eyes that remind me of his mother's.

"I'll make sure I coach every one of you boys' teams at some point, but we'll have to take turns. Plus, Uncle Cade will be coaching Micah, and you guys will be on his team. Maybe I'll be the assistant."

Sam smiles and nods.

The boys are happy I'm home for good, retired from my life as a player and commentator. I'm still adjusting. One thing I am happy about is being in Clara's bed every night. Waking up to her every morning. That sure has its perks.

By the time we pick out the presents and meet Clara and the other two boys, Isaiah is pouting and Clara has him pulled close to her, whispering something to him. But we all know what the look on her face means.

"Oh, Mom's mad," Sam says.

"Yeah. You two go stand by Luke."

"It doesn't matter if it's a girl or boy," I hear her say.

My forehead wrinkles. What the hell is she talking about?

"I want a boy!" Isaiah stomps his foot.

"You don't get to decide, and it shouldn't matter," Clara whispers in her mom tone. The one that says stop this right now or you're in big trouble. And she's not one for empty promises.

But I'm more concerned about their conversation than whatever Isaiah said to piss her off.

Isaiah crosses his arms, as defiant and stubborn as Clara can be at times.

Clara looks at me.

"Did I miss something?" I stare at her belly.

A look of confusion crosses her face before she laughs. "No. Oh my god. No! We're talking about who we have to shop for."

I blow out a breath. Thank God. I'm forty-five and not ready to start over again. We haven't done the permanent fix yet, but I think we're on the same page. Maybe I should move that up on my calendar.

I take her in my arms and hug her. "I mean, if you want—"

I'd never be able to tell Clara no if she wanted to try for a girl. When the twins came out fraternal and both boys, I felt bad for Clara. No girl to dress up or pass on her extensive library of favorite romance books. But she said she has more than enough nieces and she's meant to be a boy mom. Maybe that's the truth. I mean, she was my best friend my whole life. She could probably even coach one of their football teams and do a killer job of it. As soon as that thought goes through my head, I realize it might be the perfect idea.

We leave the toy store with the four gifts our kids picked out. Unable to handle Isaiah and his attitude, we figure Clara and I will come back by ourselves. Or order to pick it up at the store like she originally suggested. We need to get these gifts wrapped and delivered before Christmas Eve.

Isaiah gets grounded from any video games, so he doesn't talk at all during dinner, which is fine because Jaden continues to talk about me coaching his team. His excitement gets me going and wishing the season was here already.

After dinner, the boys clear the table and Clara and I clean up the dishes. We all decide to watch a Christmas movie, and Clara ends up too far away from me with our boys vying for positions by one of us. I look at her across the huge sectional and mouth, "I love you."

The boys laugh nonstop during the movie as I soak in my family, thankful for everything we have. Four healthy boys who can be trying at times, sure. But Isaiah is fast asleep on Clara's shoulder, Sam is sprawled at my feet, and with Jaden's head on my shoulder and Luke under the favorite family blanket in the chair he somehow got all to himself, I think there's not much more a guy could want than this.

"Now we have to get them all to bed," she whispers. "And I'm happy to have you here for this part."

I kiss her forehead before picking up Jaden and Isaiah. "I missed too much."

And that's the truth. Sometimes I could kick myself for being so selfish and not leaving the game the minute we had Jaden. But it was all manageable then.

"Hey." She waits until I look at her. "We did what we felt was right at the time. No regrets."

She's right, and I was grateful for having a long off-season every year. Even when I was commentating, I was able to make it home most weeks.

"I'm one lucky bastard."

She smiles. "I'm not going to argue with you there."

She gets Sam up off the floor, and he clings to her like a koala. She nudges Luke awake and he stumbles up the stairs with us.

A half hour later, I'm in our bed, waiting for Clara to join me. She comes out of the bathroom with her dark hair in a ponytail. I'm so happy she went back to her natural color after Jaden was born. I know a lot of guys like blondes, but my woman *au naturel* has always been the best.

"I had a thought today." I put down the book I'm reading, and she slides in next to me, grabbing her own book off the nightstand. This is life when your wife was the town librarian until you had kids.

"Uh-oh. What was your thought?"

"Maybe you should coach one of the boys' teams?"

She looks at me and shakes her head. "Have you seen some of those parents? They're crazy."

"You know the game better than most of the dads coaching now. I'll take Jaden, you take Luke, and Cade will coach the twins with Micah."

She smiles, and I know she likes the idea. She misses being so invested in the game too. I think she mourned my career along with me.

Her forehead wrinkles. "We'll have to ask Luke. I mean, kids can be mean."

"Once they win, I think they'll be okay with it." I place my book on the nightstand and slide closer to her.

"You're sweet-talking me." She puts her book on the nightstand and slides down under the covers to meet me.

I use the remote to turn off our light. "Have I ever thanked you properly for taking care of our family? For being the one who keeps us all in order?"

She grins. "Yes, but it never gets old."

I press my lips to hers and her arms wrap around my body. Who am I kidding? Professional football has nothing on this life.

Chapter Eleven

Chevelle

I leave Hank Jr. and Kinslee out in the backyard to play in the new snow that dropped last night and enter my dad and Marla's house. Ry is sitting at the kitchen table, an enormous plate of scrambled eggs and sausage in front of him.

"Hungry much?" I drop my bags of ornaments on the table.

"Well, since I burn off about two thousand calories in a single game, I'd say I need this much to stay alive."

I sit in a chair. "One day you're going to quit playing, and then you won't be able to eat like that."

He digs in with his fork in a dramatic fashion and shoves the food in his mouth. "And then I'll take your advice into consideration," he says around a mouthful.

"You're in a mood." I get up, seeing there's still coffee.

He doesn't say anything.

"This doesn't have anything to do with a certain brunette from Lake Starlight, does it?"

"You guys really need to get off the Calista train," he says, burying his face in his plate, unwilling to make eye contact.

I chuckle. "You don't read Buzz Wheel, do you?"

He moves to pick up his phone.

"Nope, twenty-four hours only. You missed it."

He gulps down orange juice. "What did it say?"

"How much is it worth to you?" I hold out my hand.

"Screw you, Cam is making bank. Those Five Seas boats are everywhere now. I was in San Diego and some guy started bragging about how he got his after waiting for a year."

I laugh. "I know. My husband is amazing." I bat my eyelashes.

He rolls his eyes. But Cam has an entire warehouse for his boats now. He still guarantees that every one is handmade with his care, so it keeps the brand from expanding too big, but it also drives up prices. And since the kids have gotten older, I've taken on more fishing excursions again, so we've found ourselves in a pretty comfortable financial position.

"Hey, you." My dad comes in and kisses my cheek.

"How's Marla?"

"She's actually getting better. Sitting up and watching television now. But I told her she doesn't want to push it and be down for Christmas Day, so she's staying upstairs."

I raise my eyebrows. "You do know she used to catch a cold and still carpool, volunteer, and get dinner on the table, right?"

Moms don't usually get time to lie in bed when they're feeling crappy.

"Yes, but now she can rest, so I'm making her." My dad goes over to the sink. "What's in the bags?"

"The ornament-making kits. Everyone's coming over today to make them and wrap the gifts for the underprivileged."

"Seriously?" Rylan asks.

"What? You making another trip to…"

Rylan narrows his eyes, daring me to finish that sentence. I hold out my palm and he shakes his head.

"Can't you stick around today, Rylan? You've been gone almost every day since you've been back." My dad leans against the counter and crosses his arms.

I raise my eyebrows, and Rylan inhales and exhales a loud breath.

"I'm around today, Dad. Everyone knows Chevelle needs help when it comes to the kids."

I shake my head in disgust, and Rylan laughs, continuing to scroll through his phone and eat his eggs.

"I have Cam. He's meeting me here," I say.

"Hey, Greenes!" At that moment, Cam walks in through the garage door. He looks at me and kisses my cheek. "You know that Hank Jr. is burying Kinslee in the snow, right?" He puts his hand out for my dad to shake, then turns his attention to Rylan. "Heard a little something about you, buddy."

"I told him." I grin at my little brother.

"What is it?" my dad asks, peering into the fridge.

We both look at Rylan, and he shakes his head.

"I think the kids need an adult out there," I look over Rylan's shoulder to see Hank Jr. pulling Kinslee in a sled.

"I think they want to go sledding," Cam says, cringing.

"Fucking Buzz Wheel," Rylan murmurs and stands. "I'm taking them to that big hill by the school."

"Oh, they'll love it, Ry!"

He flips me off behind Dad's back.

"Make sure to have them back within an hour though, because everyone else will be here to do ornaments."

Rylan gives me a captain salute with his middle finger again and heads upstairs to get his stuff, I assume.

My dad sits in his spot, pushing away Rylan's empty dish. "So, tell me, what's up with you two?"

I stand and unpack the bags, having to get the cement ready for all the kids' handprints. And knowing my family, the grown-ups will want to do one too. I just hope we have enough time for these to dry so we can paint them on Christmas Eve and display them on the tree.

"Not much." Cam yawns. He's been working nonstop until last night when the boat he was working on was finished. It's for my dad, a gift from all the kids. Dad's finally going to stop working and retire, so we figured why not get him a nice fishing boat to enjoy some time on the water? I think even Marla will enjoy it. "Just filling orders."

"I'm glad business is going well for you." Dad sips his coffee. "Well, I gotta get going. I have a list of things to buy for Christmas. I'll be back shortly for the ornament making."

"Sounds good, Dad."

He leaves the house and I take it upon myself to do the dishes in the sink.

Cam comes along behind me. "You got out of bed too early this morning," he whispers in my ear.

"I had about a million things to do." I turn toward him. "I got flowers for Gunner's spot. Seemed we should."

He hugs me tighter. Gunner's been gone for five years. We're grateful we had him as long as we did, but Cam's been reluctant to get another dog. Says it's not worth how much it hurts when they go. But our kids have been begging me to surprise him, so Christmas morning, a black Labrador puppy will be in a box, ready for Cam to open. Thankfully, the family of the dog that had puppies is willing to hold him until then. Now I have to recruit one of my family members to deliver him to us, so Cam doesn't get suspicious. I may have to blackmail Rylan again.

His hands slide up my sweater and cup my breasts. "We have an hour."

"Did you forget Marla is upstairs?"

"We could go to the basement. You know Rylan's done it down there before."

I turn off the water and wipe my hands while turning around. Cam cages me in, his lips falling to my neck. It's been a while for us, since Cam had to let Hank Jr. watch that stupid scary movie at Halloween. He's been in our bed more lately than when he was an infant.

"Okay, but be quiet." I take his hand and we head toward the basement.

I pull the door shut and flip the lock. His hands are all

over me on the way down the stairs and we're barely at the couch when he grabs the hem of my sweater and pulls it over my head.

For the next hour, Cam gives me the perfect Christmas present—himself. Well, and three amazing orgasms. He's a giver, what can I say?

I walk up my dad and Marla's driveway with Allie next to me and our twins in tow. "Do they not realize I have a city to protect?"

"No one does this anymore, Mom, and what if someone sees us?" Laurie whines. "I mean, how embarrassing."

"I'm not singing," Axel adds his two cents.

Allie stops and turns around, facing all of us before we head inside. From the looks of it, the majority of my family is already nestled in the nice, heated house.

"Listen, you three. We were given the easiest task of all. To pick Christmas songs to sing while we carol. We do this every year, and it's expected. I don't think I have to tell you that being a Greene in Sunrise Bay means something. Your father is the sheriff, your uncle is the state senator, and your uncles and aunts are all business owners. So please stop complaining because I don't want to hear it." Her eyes rest on me a beat longer, conveying that she shouldn't have to tell me this. "Now, we're all going to go in there with big smiles on our faces. Got it?"

She points and we follow like little ducklings with their mama. What can I say? I married a badass bitch.

We get inside, and everyone is either wrapping gifts or imprinting their hand in a ceramic ornament. Sometimes I wonder how on earth I survived this family.

Everyone is excited or they feigns excitement when they see us. The woman all gush over Allie's new hairdo. She's cut it off, and although she still looks hot as ever, there's not a lot for me to grab hold of during sex.

Leaving her in the kitchen with my sisters and sisters-in-law, I head toward the dining room, where my brothers and brothers-in-law are helping their children put their hands in the clay to capture their handprints.

This is when I'm thankful my twins are thirteen and a half.

"Axel. Laurie. Grab one and put your handprint in it."

Laurie whispers something to Althea and Shay. Three thirteen-year-olds with attitudes that make you question why you had kids to begin with. Morgan, Cade's daughter who is twelve, is right there with them too.

"We got it, Dad," Axel says and grabs one of the trays. Chevelle is managing the process and he kisses his aunt on the cheek like he should.

"He's almost got you," she says across the room, referring to my son's height.

What the hell is she talking about? Axel is not almost taller than me.

I give her a sour look. "No, he doesn't."

The guys look at me and laugh.

"Beer?" Cam asks.

"Please." I follow him into the kitchen, and we take our beers into the family room.

"You don't have to…" I thumb in the direction of the dining room.

"No, we did Kinslee's already, and she's in the basement playing with the others who are done. Hank Jr. can handle his own." He takes a pull of his beer. "So, what's going on with you?"

I shake my head. "Other than Allie cutting her hair, my son thinks he's God's gift to football now that he won a youth football conference. Oh, and according to Laurie, I have no idea what it's like to be a teenager in this day and age. As if I'd want to go back to being a teenager anyway."

"Thirteen is an evil age. I heard Posey is really struggling with Shay. Gavin said they're constantly at each other's throats."

"Laurie seems to have more of an issue with me than with Allie. It's embarrassing to her that I'm the sheriff, that I have tattoos, that I have to wear a brown uniform… I could go on and on."

"Fuck, man, I don't want Kinslee to age. She still loves her daddy." He shakes his head and takes another pull from his beer.

"Enjoy it. It changes on a dime."

We drink our beers and pretty soon, all the dads end up in the family room. We talk about football and who predicts who will make it to the Super Bowl. For a moment, I'm not upset that I'm out of my house on a work night. That is, until Allie runs her fingers through my hair and leans down to whisper it's time. I look around the room. Sure as shit, most of the women are in here to get their husbands.

We all groan but stand, finishing off our beers because we'll be taking fresh ones on our caroling trip.

"I fucking hate this," Jed mumbles.

"Whoever came up with this tradition?" Cade asks.

After we all have a fresh beer in hand, we wait while the women get all the kids into their outdoor clothes. Midway through wrestling with Clara and Xavier's son, Sam, to get his boots on, Allie looks at us.

"Do any of the dads want to help?" she asks with an arched brow.

I point at my kids, who have their jackets and hats on. "Mine are all taken care of." She narrows her eyes, so I set my beer on the table. "Come on, Sam, help your uncle out."

A lifetime later, I feel as though I ran a marathon, overheated from being dressed for outside but struggling to get kids into their gear. Allie passes out the music, hands me the stereo, and all the Greenes head out to bring some Christmas cheer to Sunrise Bay. Dad stays back with Marla so she's not lonely.

We're at the end of the driveway when I realize my beer is inside.

"Fuck," I mumble, and Allie looks at me with raised eyebrows. I nod toward the house. "My beer, babe."

Cam elbows me and hands me one he had in his coat. And that's why I love my best friend.

We all sing at the first house, and it goes well. The kids chime in, the people laugh, we laugh.

Continuing on, we get to the third house, and we've lost some of the kids to a snowball fight, the guys are having their own conversation, and the women are doing all the caroling.

An hour later, parents are chasing kids, teenagers are having major attitudes, the guys are singing obnoxiously because everyone brought a few extra beers. Turns out I'm not the bad influence on my family.

We stop at a fork in the road, deciding whether or not we should call it quits.

"Marla would be upset. She usually has us go out for three hours at least." Allie bites her lip.

Cade pulls the keys to Truth and Dare out of his pocket and jingles them.

"I like the way you think," Cam says.

"Cam," Chevelle whines.

The women act as though they're disappointed, but soon everyone agrees this is not working out and we all head downtown to Truth and Dare Brewery. We sing the entire way into town and a few passersby even smile.

Once Cade opens the door to their flagship brewery, everyone is ready to sit down and take off their layers of clothes. With a stack of coats, mittens, scarves, hats, and even the kids' boots covering a table, some people go into the kitchen and others prepare drinks. The kids get kiddie cocktails and the adults their drink of choice.

We sit at the tables, shooting the shit and spending some time together that we rarely get to enjoy.

Later that evening, after we've eaten and drank enough, I take stock around the table. Chevelle is on Cam's lap. Cade and Jed are sitting on stools behind their wives, who each have a child fast asleep in their lap. Mandi leans against Noah and his hand runs along her arm as they talk to Adam about Trey's father's sudden appearance.

Allie leans in and whispers in my ear, "What are you doing?"

I cradle her face and bring her to me. "How lucky are we?" I kiss her briefly even though I want to deepen it.

"This should be a tradition," she whispers.

She's right.

"Hey!" I shout and raise my drink. "How about this as our tradition? One night during the holidays, we do this. Drink, eat, and spend time shooting the shit with nothing else on the agenda?"

Everyone smiles and lifts their drinks.

"Cheers to that," Xavier says and we all clink.

I guess it's never too late to start new holiday traditions.

Of course, it's all fun and games until Dad and Marla walk in. Fuck. I feel like I did in high school when I'd sneak back into the house after being grounded and my dad would be sitting on the couch.

Guess some things never change.

Chapter Thirteen

Marla

Only a mother knows the strength it took me to stay upstairs in my room all week, pretending to be sick. I mean, I *was* sick, but it was only a twenty-four-hour thing. Hank caught on to my game pretty quickly, so I had no choice but to bring him into my plan.

The fact is, I'm seventy-three years old. I can't do these holidays forever. The kids need to know how to make the recipes for the foods they love, along with everything else I've incorporated since our two families blended together. When I'm gone, they'll be the ones continuing the traditions with their kids.

I'd hoped it would turn out the way it has—that they would ditch some traditions and maybe make new ones.

"Don't your mother and I get a drink?" Hank says.

"Grandpa!" Sam runs over to Hank. "I just beat Jaden at Connect Four."

They high-five together.

"Dad?" Cade flies off his stool.

The rest of the kids straighten in their seats as though we're their keepers. They're all adults.

"Mom? You feel better?" Rylan asks, coming over to me.

I've felt bad because I know what a worrier he is. Especially after being the only child home when Hank had cancer all those years ago.

"I'm good, thanks, sweetie," I say and kiss his cheek. "Go get Mom a beer."

"Sure thing. Dad?"

"Whatever your mom is having." Hank winks at me.

Rylan disappears behind the bar.

"What are we missing?" Jed asks, already knowing something is up.

Logan gets out of his chair for me and stands behind Nikki.

"Thank you," I say.

"You were never sick, were you?" Nikki asks.

"I was, but it didn't last long. I was all better about a day later."

Isaiah crawls onto my lap, resting his head on my chest. I run my hand down his back.

"But the plans were already in the works. Hank told me how everything was taken care of. So I thought it was about time you all learned how to pull off a Christmas. And you've done it beautifully. I'm upset I missed so much of the execution, but had I been there, it wouldn't have happened."

The kids nod because they know I'm right. I've done everything for this family since we came together and I would never take it back, but they each have families of their own now. And I'm way too old to continue doing all of it.

"We cut the caroling short," Mandi admits, never able to lie.

"I know. And that's okay. Caroling is my thing and this"—I look around and kiss the top of Isaiah's head—"is yours."

"What do you mean?" Adam asks, coming a little closer.

"This can be your tradition."

"Do you have a nanny cam in here?" Adam looks around. "We just said it was going to be our new tradition."

I laugh. "No. But traditions usually come from moments like this—when you had no plans to start one and stumble upon something you all enjoy. That's what makes the best kind of traditions." I sip my beer Rylan just set in front of me. "Is it okay that your dad and I intrude?"

I look at Hank, who is with the grandkids and talking about how the caroling fell apart. All the teenagers think it's funny.

"We want you here with us." Nikki puts her hand on mine. "I'm glad you're not sick. You didn't have to go to these lengths to trick us."

I scrunch up my nose. "Hmm… I think I did."

"Okay, so now that you're not sick and you're here, I need to talk to you about Logan," Nikki whispers, leaning in across the table.

"And Mom, Shay has been a bear. How did you handle us at that age?" Posey whines.

"Maisie doesn't believe in Santa anymore, Mom," Mandi whispers.

"Trey's biological father is in Sunrise Bay," Lucy says with tears in her eyes.

"Xavier wants me to coach Luke's football team next year." Clara looks excited by the prospect.

"I'm convinced Cade's about to go through a midlife crisis," Presley says.

I hold up my hands. "Okay, girls, guess what?"

They all look at me, and I can't deny it feels good knowing how much they want my advice. And I want to guide them, but they have to navigate these curveballs life throws their way themselves.

"You will all figure out the solutions yourself. You don't need me."

"We do," Allie says next to me.

I shake my head. "You were all about to pull off Christmas on your own. You know the good thing about having a big family? You have a huge network of people who love you and can help guide and support you." I look at Molly. "Remember when Emelia was no picnic?"

"Boy, do I." She rolls her eyes.

"Help Posey with some solutions."

I continue to pair them all up with someone else in the family who can help them, and after we're done and laughing at something one of the kids did, Nikki leans in close.

"Are you sick?" she whispers.

"No." I shake my head.

"Then why did you do it?" I knew she'd be the one who wouldn't understand why I pretended to be sick.

"I felt it was time to hand over the reins."

"But now we can't come to you for advice?"

"You still can. I'm still here, but I want you guys to see that you have more than just me. You have one another." She lays her head on my shoulder and I wrap my arm around my oldest daughter, kissing the top of her head. "I love you, Nik."

"I love you too, Mom. Promise me you'll live forever?"

I laugh and catch Hank's gaze across the room. "I can't promise that, but I can promise you'll be okay whenever the time comes."

"Let's make a toast!" Hank comes over to where I sit. "Thirty-one years ago, a woman and her four kids showed up in Sunrise Bay and changed mine and my five kids' lives forever. Then we added another one to the mix."

Everyone smiles at Rylan.

"You mean accidentally added another," Jed says and puts his arm around Rylan.

"Regardless, two Greene families were brought together until death do they part. You've all given me such a gift, my heart overflows with happiness. Thank you to everyone, but especially my girl. You always know what our family needs, and it makes me love you even more." Hank raises his glass while tears build in my eyes, and we all clink them before taking our sips.

"This is definitely the good life," I say and give Hank a kiss.

Everyone clinks their glasses again.

I look over the group. "And now we all need to get back home and finish wrapping those gifts so we can deliver them."

They laugh but soon realize I'm not joking. I guess my job will never be done while I'm still around, but at least I know they'll always take care of one another.

Chapter Fourteen

Ethel

I'm not sure how I got picked to write the Christmas card. Maybe because I'm an old fart and not as mobile as I used to be. As I sit in the den of what used to be my house, the house my precious Jim built for me, I write the Christmas update that will be inserted in the card. Guess it'll have to be a New Year's Eve card now.

Merry Christmas, everyone! Ethel Greene here with a little update on the family. I'm still at Northern Lights Retirement Center with friends while the rest of my family resides in Sunrise Bay.

My son, Hank, and his wife, Marla, are enjoying being empty nesters. Hank is finally retiring, and Marla is trying to take up knitting because the woman is convinced that's what old people do. If she'd just take a card from me and my friends, I think she'd be much happier. We aren't the knitting kind of grandmas and I like to think we live a better life for it.

Cade and his wife, Presley, have two daughters, Leighton and Morgan, along with a boy named Micah. Cade's having a bit of an issue with the idea that he's getting older, but once he settles into the idea, he'll realize it's actually much better. There's this thing that happens when you age where you just don't care that much what other people think and it's divine.

Jed and his wife, Molly, have Emelia, who's in college and has a boyfriend we all hope to meet next week, along with their son and daughter, Joshua and Peyton. Jed is finally having to reckon with the fact that his oldest daughter likes guys a lot, just like he liked a bunch of girls back in the day. I always told him his wandering ways would come back to bite him in the you-know-what.

Fisher and Allie have the twins, Axel and Laurie. I wouldn't want to be in that house with the two of them going through puberty right now. Word on the street—or in the home, as it were—is that Laurie is giving Fisher a run for his money. Just desserts I think, given all the gray hair he gave his dad as a teen.

Nikki and Logan have three boys, Noah, Crew, and Wade. We have three little soon-to-be MMA stars in our future. Then again, maybe not if Nikki has anything to say about it.

Mandi and Noah have Maisie, and those three are very happy traveling the world and running SunBay Inn. Maisie questioned her belief in Santa this year but ate her words when her Uncle Rylan asked if she wanted to chance not getting a gift because she doesn't believe. Mandi's crossing her fingers she'll keep believing until next year now.

Xavier retired from commentating this year, and his permanent residence is in Sunrise Bay. He and Clara, along with their four boys, Jaden, Luke, Isaiah, and Sam, will be busy next fall when the youth football season starts, and Clara has decided to be the first female coach in the local league for Luke's team. Us Greene women know how to get things done.

Adam and Lucy's family has grown. No, not with another kid. Trey decided to find his birth parents, and his biological father joined us for Christmas dinner. There's always room at our table for more, and though they were a little shocked at first, Adam and Lucy made sure to let Trey know his bio parents are always welcome. Althea was more than happy to be at the kids' table with her thirteen-year-old cousins. I overheard a lot about boys, some app on their phone called Tip Tap or something, and some book they've all been reading and passing around.

Posey is still keeping everyone in Sunrise Bay stylish with her hair salon, Fringe, and Gavin is now a senator for the state of Alaska. We're all hoping Shay makes it to her fourteenth birthday. Her attitude with Posey doesn't make it look promising. Little Kiera continues to be a sweet angel.

Chevelle is finally running charters again, and Cam's business is thriving. They welcomed a new dog this Christmas, which Cam is pretending not to enjoy, but he can't stop picking the thing up. Their kids, Hank Jr. and Kinslee, agreed to name the new dog Mystic. We're pretty sure he'll be getting trained just like Gunner, may he rest in peace.

The baby of the family, Rylan, isn't a baby anymore. He's the last one who remains single. Maybe because he's too busy playing professional soccer and traveling the world. His time is coming though. Luckily, he's an easy case because he's already found the love of his life and we know she loves him too. The trouble is convincing the two of them to weather this storm we call life together, that they're more powerful together than apart. He's convinced himself he's doing great, but everyone close to him knows that's a lie. He needs her.

As for me, I'm getting up there. As soon as you realize you're closer to death than you are to living, you thank the universe every day you open your eyes. You take stock of your life. What you did right and what you might rewrite if you had the ability. Truth is, I've had a good life. It's been full of love and friendship and family. What more could an old girl ask for?

I wouldn't change anything. Sure, I wish some people didn't have to die. I wish my Jim would've lived to meet his grandkids and great-grandchildren. To help his son through the death of his first wife. To witness the way Marla filled that void and gave Hank hope that he wouldn't mourn Laurie for the rest of his life.

The merging of two families isn't easy for anyone, but when I look at how everyone treats one another as true sisters and brothers, it makes me proud. It's been a beautiful thing to witness. Knowing that I've had something to do with each of my grandkids finding their spouse brings me immense satisfaction. Nine down and one to go. I need to figure out Rylan sooner rather than later.

We're fortunate that everyone is happy and healthy. Sure, we have some problems, no family is without them, but I like to think we grow with each one.

Merry Christmas, everyone, from the Greenes to you!

Chapter Fifteen

Calista

I t's three days past Christmas as I sit in the uncomfortable plastic chair at the airport. I knew Rylan would get out of Alaska before New Year's Eve. I can't help but wonder about his plans. Has he asked a woman to be his date to some big charity party? Or is he going to a private party with celebrities where he's sure to kiss the most beautiful woman in the room at midnight? Each thought feels like someone's pushing the tip of a knife deeper into my heart.

He's wearing jeans and a Henley, his jacket hanging on his carry-on as he makes his way to security. He'll be out of my sight soon and there's no saying when I'll see him again. Maybe never.

When he glances in my direction, I pick up the book I'm pretending to read. My disguise of Dion's blond wig from when he was Axel Rose for Halloween should keep me off Rylan's radar. Every step he takes farther away, I want to stand and announce myself. But that's not good for either of us.

He puts his stuff on the conveyor and removes his shoes. He has a warm smile for the security attendant who asks him a couple questions. He says something to make her laugh and jealousy pricks me. Then he's putting on his shoes.

This is the last moment I have to soak him in. I stand, needing just one moment longer.

He swings his carry-on over his shoulder and walks away without a glance.

Mission accomplished—see him off without him seeing me. But why does it always feel so unfinished? For just once, I'd like to feel as though the past is sealed and put away as it should be.

I look one last time and a part of me hopes he's there, but he isn't. He's lost in the throes of people walking to their gates.

Goodbye, Rylan Greene.

The End

also by piper rayne

The Baileys

Lessons from a One-Night Stand (FREE)

Advice from a Jilted Bride

Birth of a Baby Daddy

Operation Bailey Wedding (Novella)

Falling for My Brother's Best Friend

Demise of a Self-Centered Playboy

Confessions of a Naughty Nanny

Operation Bailey Babies (Novella)

Secrets of the World's Worst Matchmaker

Winning my Best Friend's Girl

Rules for Dating Your Ex

Operation Bailey Birthday (Novella)

The Greene Family

My Twist of Fortune (Free Prequel)

My Beautiful Neighbor (FREE)

My Almost Ex

My Vegas Groom

A Greene Family Summer Bash (Novella)

My Sister's Flirty Friend

My Unexpected Surprise

My Famous Frenemy

A Greene Family Vacation (Novella)

My Scorned Best Friend

My Fake Fiancé

My Brother's Forbidden Friend

A Greene Family Christmas (Novella)

Lake Starlight

The Problem with Second Chances

The Issue with Bad Boy Roommates

The Trouble with Runaway Brides

The Drawback of Single Dads

Plain Daisy Ranch

One Last Summer

The One I Left Behind

The One I Stood Beside

The One I Didn't See Coming

Modern Love

Charmed by the Bartender

Hooked by the Boxer

Mad about the Banker

Single Dads Club

Real Deal

Dirty Talker

Sexy Beast

Hollywood Hearts

Mister Mom

Animal Attraction

Domestic Bliss

Bedroom Games

Cold as Ice

On Thin Ice

Break the Ice

Chicago Law

Smitten with the Best Man

Tempted by my Ex-Husband

Seduced by my Ex's Divorce Attorney

Blue Collar Brothers

Flirting with Fire

Crushing on the Cop

Engaged to the EMT

White Collar Brothers

Sexy Filthy Boss

Dirty Flirty Enemy

Wild Steamy Hook-up

The Rooftop Crew

My Bestie's Ex

A Royal Mistake

The Rival Roomies

Our Star-Crossed Kiss

The Do-Over

A Co-Workers Crush

Hockey Hotties

Countdown to a Kiss (Free Prequel)

My Lucky #13 (FREE)

The Trouble with #9

Faking it with #41

Tropical Hat Trick (Novella)

Sneaking around with #34

Second Shot with #76

Offside with #55

Kingsmen Football Stars

False Start (Free Prequel)

You Had Your Chance, Lee Burrows

You Can't Kiss the Nanny, Brady Banks

Over My Brother's Dead Body, Chase Andrews

Chicago Grizzlies

On the Defense (Free Prequel)

Something like Hate

Something like Lust

Something like Love

The Nest

Mr. Heartbreaker

Mr. Broody

Mr. S (Title to be revealed)

Mr. C (Title to be revealed)

Holiday Romances

Single and Ready to Jingle

Claus and Effect

Merry Kissmas

Cockamamie Unicorn Ramblings

A lot of changes happened in the twelve years since Cam and Chevelle's book, right?

We love doing the novellas and giving you glimpses of the characters in the future, plus dropping any easter eggs about upcoming books. Ahem... Calista and Rylan, anyone?

Thank you to everyone who read this entire series! We have the most awesome readers who keep us going and there's no way to show you the level of appreciation we have in our hearts. When we set out to write the Baileys, we never thought we'd finish another nine-book series afterward about another Alaska family but we're so glad we did!

As always, we have a lot of people to thank for getting this book into your hands...

Nina and the entire Valentine PR team.
Cassie from Joy Editing for line edits.
Ellie from My Brother's Editor for line edits.
Rosa from My Brother's Editor for proofreading.
Hang Le for the cover and branding for the entire series.
Bloggers who consistently carve out time to read, review and/or promote us.
Piper Rayne Unicorns who give us a safe space online to chat and show us love on the daily!
Readers who took the time to read our story and champion this series to other readers. We are grateful beyond words for your support and excited for what's next with our Alaska families!

Heading into the Lake Starlight series we're going to stay

in the time period we're in right now. Actually, for Calista and Rylan's book we're going to push it one more year out. We hope you'll join us when the Bailey grand kids get their own series, Lake Starlight.

xo,
Piper & Rayne

about piper & rayne

Piper Rayne is a USA Today Bestselling Author duo who write "heartwarming humor with a side of sizzle" about families, whether that be blood or found. They both have e-readers full of one-clickable books, they're married to husbands who drive them to drink, and they're both chauffeurs to their kids. Most of all, they love hot heroes and quirky heroines who make them laugh, and they hope you do, too!